TEDDY BEAR
STORIES
and RHYMES

Contents

Material in this edition was previously published
in *Teddy Bear Tales*.

A catalogue record for this book is available from the British Library

Published by Ladybird Books Ltd
A subsidiary of the Penguin Group
A Pearson Company
© LADYBIRD BOOKS LTD MCMXCVII

LADYBIRD and the device of a Ladybird are trademarks of
Ladybird Books Ltd Loughborough Leicestershire UK

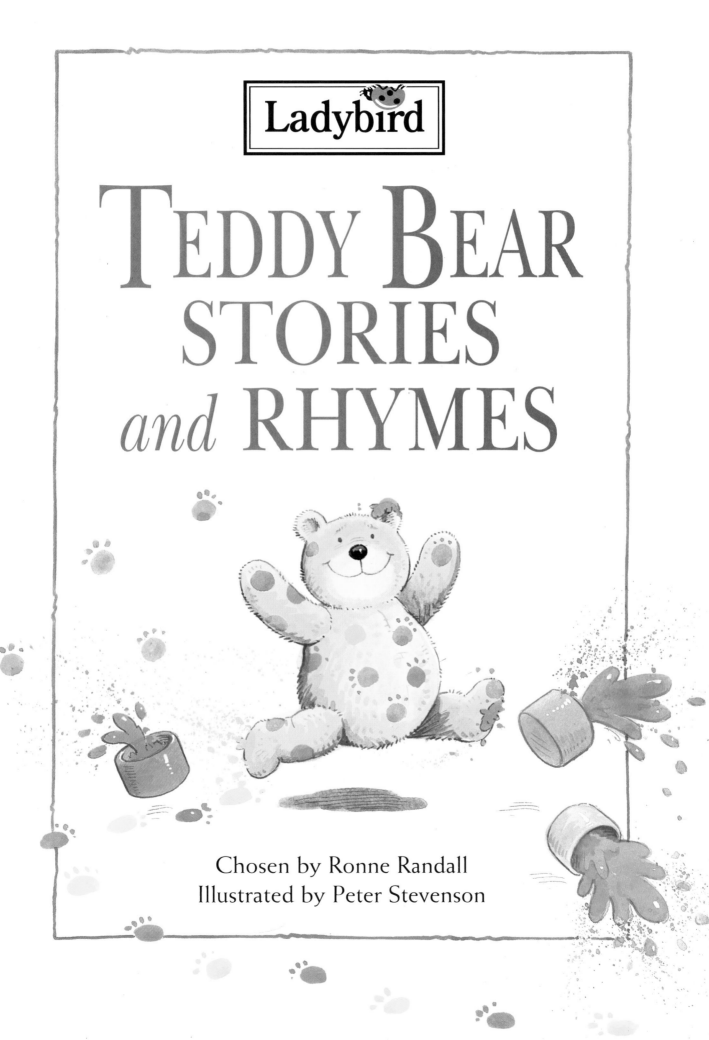

TEDDY BEAR
STORIES
and RHYMES

Chosen by Ronne Randall
Illustrated by Peter Stevenson

Edward's First Party

Edward stood on his head. Next he turned a cartwheel. Then he simply sat on his bed and squirmed.

Tomorrow Edward was going to his first Teddy Bear Party.

Fabulous food! Great games! And lots of new bears to meet! he thought to himself.

But then Edward gave a little frown. Because Edward's owner, Tina, had been invited, too. And Tina had *terrible* table manners.

Edward began to fret.

"What if Tina rushes at her food? What if she chatters with her mouth full? And what if… oh no!…" Edward blushed at the thought. *What if Tina gets her horrible hiccups?*

Next morning Edward woke up feeling excited and anxious all at once.

Tina was excited, too. At breakfast she told Dad all about the party. And, although she ate an egg, toast, cereal and orange juice, she didn't stop talking once.

At lunch Tina lunged for the sauce. Then she gobbled down her meal and rushed upstairs to choose her party clothes.

Then Edward heard her, all the way from downstairs.

"Hic-hic! Hic-hic!"

"Oh no!" groaned Edward. "There she goes!"

Mum made Tina drink a glass of water upside down. Then Mum, Tina and Edward walked very gently to the party. Edward kept his paws crossed all the way.

But just as Mum rang the doorbell – "Hic!" – Tina got hiccups again. Edward didn't know where to put himself.

At last the door opened. Edward was almost too embarrassed to go inside. But when he did, Edward couldn't believe his eyes – or his ears!

Because all the bear owners were rushing at their food. They all seemed to be shrieking as they ate. And, to Edward's delight, every single owner had… hiccups!

My Bear

I'd like to be a pilot
And hurtle through the air,
But even if I looped the loop,
I still would need my bear.

I'd like to be a jockey
And ride a frisky mare,
But even if I won the race
I still would need my bear.

I'd like to be a gymnast
And dangle for a dare,
But even if I wowed the crowd,
I still would need my bear.

I'd like to be a pop star
With rings and purple hair,
But even if I made you scream,
I still would need my bear.

I'd like to be a teacher–
What lessons I'd prepare!
But even if I knew it all,
I still would need my bear.

It's fun to plan and daydream,
It's better still to share.
So even when he's old and worn,
I still will need my bear.

My Owner

My owner has a rumply bed,
She sometimes doesn't wash!
But even when she snores or squirms,
I never mind a squash.

"Let's play a game," she sometimes cries,
And, "Teddy, you begin."
But sometimes when we play a game,
I *wish* she'd let me win!

My owner sometimes stamps and shouts
(She's not a pretty sight!),
But even when the grown-ups glare,
I'm there to hold her tight.

My owner likes to go on trips
By boat or train or bus.
And if I didn't go as well,
I know there'd be a fuss.

We have our ups and downs of days,
But still we both agree,
I wouldn't change her for the world,
And nor would she change me.

No Fun Fair for Freddy

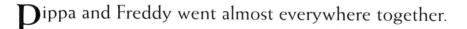

Pippa and Freddy went almost everywhere together.

But Pippa was a girl who easily became excited and… forgetful!

"Where's Freddy?" Mum would say at bedtime. And then there would be a frantic search.

Freddy had been left everywhere, from the library to the swimming pool.

In the end, Mum made him a special badge. On it were his name, address and telephone number. And kind people were always either delivering Freddy to the door or telephoning for him to be collected.

One day, Pippa was particularly excited. A fun fair was coming to town the following week! But, right from the start, Mum was firm.

"No fun fair for Freddy," she announced. "It wouldn't be safe. It wouldn't be sensible. Freddy might get lost or squashed in no time at all."

All week Pippa argued. And the day before the fun fair, she decided to make a *huge* effort.

"If I show Mum that I can be really responsible," Pippa told herself, "then perhaps Freddy can come to the fun fair after all."

That afternoon, Pippa, Freddy and Mum set off for the shops.
On the way, they delivered a parcel to Mike's mum.

"Come in," she said. "Mike's building a spaceship."

Pippa clutched Freddy firmly as she raced up the stairs.

"Oooh!" squealed Pippa, when she saw the kit. "Can I help?"

The two friends had a terrific time together. But just as Mum and
Pippa were leaving, Mike's mum came running after them.

"Don't forget Freddy," she cried kindly,
"or he might fly to the moon without you!"

Pippa blushed. Mum didn't say a word. But Pippa knew exactly what she was thinking: "No fun fair for Freddy!"

When they reached the supermarket, it was even busier than usual. While Mum pushed the trolley, Pippa gave all her attention to Freddy.

But just before the checkout there was a special display.

"Oooh!" squealed Pippa. "It's my favourite snack!" And she rushed forward to load the trolley.

Pippa and Mum chatted happily as they left the store. But suddenly the manager came running after them.

"Don't forget your teddy," he cried kindly, "or he might eat too many Crunchy Crisp-O-s!"

Mum didn't say a word. But Pippa muttered miserably, "No fun fair for Freddy!"

On the way home, Pippa, Freddy and Mum stopped off at the park.

Pippa pushed Freddy carefully on the swings. They whizzed down the slide in a bear hug.

But suddenly Pippa caught sight of Katie.

"Oooh!" squealed Pippa. "Do you want to play hide-and-seek with me?"

At last Mum and Pippa waved goodbye. But then a big boy came running after them.

"Hey!" he called. "Don't forget your bear, or he might get trampled in our game!"

When they got home, Pippa threw herself on her bed. "I don't want to go to the fun fair," she wailed. "Not without Freddy!"

All night long, Pippa tried not to think about the fun fair. But pictures of exciting rides and wonderful things to eat kept filling her dreams.

In the morning, Pippa rummaged on her tousled bed. "Where's Freddy?" she asked sleepily.

And then Pippa saw him.

Freddy was perched on the shelf, looking pleased with himself. He was smartly dressed… in Pippa's old baby sling!

"One of my better brain waves," said Mum, smiling proudly.

And, as soon as she had adjusted the straps to fit Pippa perfectly, Freddy was… all set for the fun fair!

Marcus and Lionel

Marcus and Lionel had been together for as long as they could remember. They lived on the little girl's bed, propped up against her pillow.

Marcus often went places with the little girl. And when he got home, he always told Lionel about his adventures. Lionel was too big to travel, and never got to go anywhere. Sometimes he wished he could have an adventure of his own, but most of the time he was content to sit on the bed and hear about the world outside.

One summer morning, there was lots of bustle and clatter in the house. People had come with boxes for packing things, and there was a van to take everything away. The little girl and her parents were moving to the countryside.

Marcus was going to ride in the
car. But Lionel was packed in a box,
along with the pillows and some
blankets. He just had time to say
goodbye to Marcus before the
lid was shut.

Marcus had a wonderful journey.
There was so much to see! They
rode through busy city streets, one
after the other.

Then they came to a big bridge. Marcus had never
seen a bridge before. *Wait until I tell Lionel about this!* he thought.

As they crossed the bridge, Marcus saw boats in the water. When
they got to the other side, he saw hills and a windmill and cows
in fields.

I can't wait to tell Lionel! he thought.

At last they arrived at the new house. There were trees at the front, and swings and a slide at the back. The little girl's bedroom looked out over a garden with red roses growing in it.

Lionel and I will be happy here, Marcus thought.

The little girl and her parents started to unpack the boxes. Marcus could hardly wait to see Lionel.

They unpacked the little girl's clothes, and all her books. They unpacked her doll's house and her cowboy hat and boots. There was no sign of Lionel yet.

They unpacked the tea set, the easel and the bedside lamp. There was still no sign of Lionel.

There was only one box left. *Lionel* has *to be in that one,* Marcus thought.

But he wasn't. It was only the little girl's games and jigsaws.

That night, the little girl had to sleep with her mother's pillow—and no Lionel. She hugged Marcus extra tight, and Marcus tried hard to hug her back.

"I'm sure Lionel will turn up," he thought. But Lionel didn't.

Over the next few days, Marcus and the little girl had lots of new things to explore. There were trees to climb, and a little stream with frogs and fish. There was a hidey-hole in one of the big trees, and there were four cats next door who came to visit.

Discovering it all should have been a great adventure for Marcus, but it wasn't much fun. Lionel wasn't there to hear about it when Marcus came home.

The days seemed very long.

One day, the little girl took Marcus out to the car. She and her mum were going to visit someone in the city, and Marcus was going, too.

On the way, Marcus saw lots of things he remembered from the moving day. That made him miss Lionel more than ever.

When they got to the city, the little girl carried Marcus in her usual way—by one arm. This always gave Marcus an interesting view of things.

And that day Marcus got a *very* interesting view of something. Behind an iron gate, on the lawn in front of a big grey building, there were tables with all sorts of things set out on display: chairs and clothes and clocks and books…

And right there, on one of those tables, was… could it be?

Yes! It was… Lionel!

Marcus had to make the little girl stop, so she would see Lionel, too. But how? She and her mum seemed to be in such a hurry!

There was only one way. Gathering all his strength, Marcus stuck out one leg—just far enough to get his foot caught in the gate.

As the little girl walked on, Marcus's foot began to tear. It hurt terribly. But it would be worth it, if only…

"Mum, wait," said the little girl, stopping. "Marcus's foot is stuck."

24

As the little girl began to free his foot, she suddenly saw what Marcus had seen.

"Mum!" she cried. "Mum, look! It's Lionel! We found him, Mum! We found Lionel!"

Indeed they had. He was a bit dusty, and one of his seams was torn, but otherwise he was fine. They got him from the jumble sale, and that afternoon they took him home to the countryside.

The little girl's mum mended his seam and gave him a bath. She mended Marcus's foot, too, so it didn't hurt any more.

Marcus and Lionel were so happy to be together again. They spent days and days catching up on all that had happened. It was just like old times.

Well, almost: now Lionel had some adventures to tell Marcus about, too!

Pawmarks

There are pawmarks on the table,
There are pawmarks on the chairs.
There are pawmarks in the hallway,
As well as up the stairs!

There are pawmarks in the bathroom,
There are pawmarks on the mat.
There are pawmarks on the aftershave –
Dad won't think much of *that*!

There are pawmarks in the bedroom,
There are pawmarks in the bed.
There are pawmarks on my nightie
In several shades of red.

Now, each and every pawmark
Came from a bear called Sid –
And all because the finger paints
Were left without a lid!

Whizz Fizz Bear

Nigel liked a night-time nibble. As soon as the house was quiet, he would creep downstairs to explore the fridge.

Nigel's favourite food was cheese. And one day Nigel's owner, Harry, popped something really tasty into the shopping trolley.

"Good heavens, Harry!" cried Dad. "This cheese is *exceptional!*"

Nigel waited impatiently for night-time. At last the house was quiet.

"Mmmm!" murmured Nigel as he sampled the latest flavour. And before he knew it, Nigel's nibble had become a mammoth meal.

Now Nigel was feeling thirsty... *very* thirsty. He delved deeper into the fridge.

"Bother!" grumbled Nigel. "This carton of orange juice is empty." But then he saw the bottle.

FUN FIZZ said the cheerful label. And then, in smaller letters, *'guaranteed to quench your thirst'*.

Nigel reached for it eagerly. He'd never managed to open a bottle by himself before. But this time he was in luck – the bottle was half empty, and the cap was loose.

Whizz, Fizz! A million bubbles tickled Nigel's nose.

Whizz, Fizz! Nigel had never tasted *anything* like it!

Very soon the bottle was empty.

But then Nigel noticed the crate. It was parked by the back door, and it was *full* of Fizz.

Nigel skipped across the kitchen. But this time he was out of luck. Because, though he tried every single bottle, he couldn't open any of them.

Reluctantly, Nigel padded back to bed. But he couldn't get the Fizz out of his mind.

Nigel tossed and turned. He'd never been so thirsty. Then, suddenly, he found himself back in the quiet kitchen again. And this time it was a different story.

"Whizz, Fizz, wow!" cried Nigel, as he opened the first bottle with ease. "Being thirsty must have made me stronger!

Whizz, Fizz! Whizz, Fizz! Nigel worked his way steadily through the crate. By the time he reached the last bottle, he was feeling light-headed, light-pawed and…

"Help!" cried Nigel. He was so full of bubbles that he had begun to float – just like a helium balloon!

First Nigel glided through the kitchen. Next he hovered in the hall. Then – *whoosh!* – he floated up the stairs and into Harry's bedroom.

"Oh no!" cried Nigel. "The window's open!"

Nigel was in a panic. He didn't want to fly off into the night. He would be heartbroken to leave his happy home and fridge.

So, with a desperate lunge, Nigel grabbed hold of Harry's bookshelf.

Crash! Down came all Harry's books. And so did Nigel.

Slowly, he opened one eye. But all Nigel could see was the familiar design on Harry's wallpaper.

Gradually, Nigel came to his senses. Then, suddenly, he gave a great *"Whoop!"*

"I didn't drink all the Fizz after all!" cried Nigel. "I've just been having a nightmare, and I've fallen out of bed."

Nigel wriggled with relief. But he was still thirsty. Then he saw the tumbler of water. Harry's dad had left it by the bed, just in case the new cheese had made Harry thirsty. Nigel drank deeply. Then he settled back into bed and a happy, dreamlike sleep.

The next day Harry's family had visitors. Harry and Nigel were on their best behaviour.

And, when the drinks were poured, Nigel shook his head politely at the Fizz.

"No thanks," he seemed to say.
"Mine's an orange juice."

It Was Teddy!

Carl was a careless little boy. But he didn't like to admit it.

So, when he turned on the taps and flooded the bathroom, he wouldn't own up. "It was Teddy!" he told his parents.

The same thing happened when Carl took an ice cream out of the freezer, and then left it to melt.

"What a waste!" said Mum.

"What a *careless* Teddy!" sighed Carl.

Then one day Carl accidentally hurled a ball through Mrs Weaver's window.

"*Naughty* Teddy!" announced naughty Carl.

"Teddy has been causing a *lot* of trouble," said Dad. So he decided to have a talk with Carl's teacher.

Now, Carl and Teddy were still new boys at school. But Carl enjoyed school, and he worked hard.

"Next week," Miss Mulberry told the children, "we are having an important visitor. I want you all to make her a nice picture."

Carl painted his best picture ever. Miss Mulberry put it up on the wall along with the others.

When the important visitor arrived, she was impressed. "What wonderful paintings!" she exclaimed. Then she took a closer look and pointed to Carl's. "Who painted *this* one?" she asked. "It's outstanding!"

Carl squirmed with pride, and Miss Mulberry smiled across the room. "It was Teddy!" she told the visitor.

That evening Carl took a glass of milk up to his bedroom. But he soon came down again.

"Sorry," said Carl. "I've spilt my milk and made a mess."

Mum and Dad looked amazed. "Who taught you to own up?" they asked.

Carl beamed at his parents. Then he told them, "It was Teddy!"

Christmas Bear

A tear rolled down Sally's cheek as her mother switched off the bedroom light. It was Christmas Eve, and Sally had forgotten to post her letter to Santa Claus. She had found it stuffed in her jacket pocket.

How would Santa know what Sally really wanted? Maybe he'd forget her altogether!

Sally and her parents had still put out two mince pies and a glass of milk to welcome Santa. The red stocking hung ready at the foot of her bed as it did every Christmas Eve. But this year Sally was sure it would remain empty.

She sniffed miserably to herself as she drifted off to sleep…

Meanwhile, a bright shape was racing through the starry sky. It was Santa Claus, riding in his biggest sleigh, pulled by his fastest reindeer!

The sleigh was filled with sacks of presents, neatly sorted and labelled for children all over the world.

But in one of the sacks something was stirring…

A little paw appeared, and then another. Then two ears, followed by a furry head and a furry body.

It was a teddy bear… a very naughty teddy bear!

The sleigh made a sudden turn. One second the teddy bear was safe inside the sack, and the next he was tumbling down, over and over and over. He gave one shrill squeak, but Santa Claus heard nothing except the rushing of the wind and the jingling of the reindeer's bells.

Over and over Bear fell, towards white fields far below.

Down…

and down…

and down he went…

until suddenly he landed in the snow-laden branches of a fir tree.

"Ouch!" he cried as he slid through the prickly branches and disappeared into a deep snowdrift.

All was still and silent and very, very cold.

Bear couldn't tell whether he was upside down or the right way up. It was some time before he pushed away the snow and found himself looking out into the night.

A little way off he saw a person dressed all in white.

"Aha!" said Bear. "*There's* someone who will help me."

He struggled to his feet and trudged through the snow, which as you can imagine seemed very deep to a little bear.

"Excuse me," he called out as he came closer. "Can you please tell me where I am?"

There was no answer from the person dressed in white.

Bear tried once more. "Excuse me," he said loudly. "Can you tell me where I am?"

Again there was no answer. The person in white didn't even look down to see who was talking.

"Well!" said Bear, turning away. "I hope all the people here aren't so rude!"

Bear was now feeling very cold and sorry for himself. He wished he was safe and snug in Santa's sack.

He sighed and looked around. Not far off there was a house. *And where there is a house*, Bear thought to himself, *there will be people and warmth*.

He walked round the house twice, trying to find a way in, but the door handles and windows were all too high for him to reach.

He was about to give up when a black cat came padding round the corner. It stopped and looked the little bear up and down, its fur bristling and its whiskers twitching. Then, deciding that bears were of no great interest, the cat turned and walked away.

The cat climbed up some steps to a closed door and then vanished completely. The last Bear saw of it was its tail disappearing through the unopened door.

A magic cat! thought Bear.

But he soon discovered that the cat had its own private cat-sized door. There in front of him was a hinged flap.

Bear reached up and pushed himself against it. The next thing he knew, he was tumbling head-first through the opening.

Bear thumped down onto a soft carpet. What bliss to be inside!

For a minute he lay still with his eyes shut, enjoying the warmth and comfort. Then he opened his eyes.

It was very dark. In front of him there was a staircase, and at the top he saw a dim light.

It's time for a good snooze, Bear thought. He'd had enough adventures for a while.

Bear dragged himself up towards the light. He was out of breath when he pulled himself up the last step.

The light was coming from an open door. From inside, Bear could hear the sound of soft breathing.

He tiptoed to the door and nearly tripped over something lying just inside. It was a plate with two mince pies on it! Next to it was a small glass of milk.

Now, Bear felt very hungry indeed. He sat himself down by the plate and ate steadily and happily until he had finished both pies.

How kind of them to think of me! Bear thought, gulping down the milk.

It was only then that he started to look around the room. In one corner there was a bed, and in it someone was sleeping peacefully.

"That's where I'd like to be," Bear whispered.

It wasn't easy getting up onto the bed, but he finally did it. A tired bear can be a very determined bear if he spots a comfortable place to sleep.

The effort was worth it. For what should he find at the end of the bed but a cosy red sleeping bag. It was just the right size!

In no time at all, he snuggled his way into it and fell fast asleep…

Sally opened her eyes. It was morning. *Christmas* morning!

But Sally's heart sank as she remembered her unposted letter to Santa.

Had he brought her anything at all? She looked towards the door. The mince pies and the milk had gone!

Quickly she crawled down to the bottom of the bed. The red stocking was no longer flat and empty. It was bulging. There really *was* something in it!

Bursting with excitement, she reached in and pulled out… a furry teddy bear!

Sally gazed at it wide-eyed. "But how could Santa have known you were exactly what I wanted?" she asked the little bear, thinking of the letter in her jacket pocket. This is what it said:

Dear Santa,
    Please can I have my very own bear for Christmas?

        Lots of love
        Sally
        xxx

Was it Sally's imagination, or did the little bear seem to smile?